# BUBBLES WITH THE PACK

## OMEGAVERSE HOLIDAY QUICKIES

### CLOVER HOLLOWAY

Book Cover: Unfortunate Designs

Independently Published by Unfortunate Productions LLC

Print ISBN: 979-8-9913742-7-9

# BLURB

Talia's New Year's resolution is to say yes more. Yes to adventure. Yes to pleasure. Yes to...love?

That's how she finds herself at a fancy party for the elite at the Manaway House. When she stumbles upon three alpha billionaires who happen to be her scent matches, Talia decides to stick to her promise and dive straight in.

*Omegaverse Holiday Quickies are novelettes with more smut than plot. They are meant to be a fun escape with no angst that you can read in one sitting. Have fun and get your spice on!*

*Champagne showers are about to get real*

# AUTHOR'S NOTE

A note about the Omegaverse Holiday Quickies series. We all love Omegaverse books with lots of character development and conflict resolution, and of course heats, but sometimes you just want a short little palate cleanser to read in between longer novels, or while you're in the waiting room at the doctor's office, or the school pick up line...you catch my drift.

That's where the Omegaverse Holiday Quickies series comes in! I love reading those short instalove/instalust where a OTT man falls hard and fast for a damsel he rescued from the woods/mountain/mafia/ex/etc, but I usually only find them in the contemporary genres. I wanted to capture that same vibe but with an Omegaverse twist.

All of these stories will be of existing packs, or insta-love pack formation, with no angst or third act breakups. They are very short, and meant to be fast, fun, and totally smutty.

They are also light on the Omegaverse pitfalls, and won't always center around a heat. The spice will be spicin' though, I promise you that! If you aren't familiar with Omegaverse, take a look at the short primer I included next.

All my books are queer. The worlds they are set in are queer-normative and there will always be a wide mix of relationship pairings, dynamics, and genders. Even if the primary relationship is a man and a woman, all my characters are pan unless otherwise stated. If that's not something you're comfortable with, my books likely aren't for you.

There are also explicit adult scenes mixed with a healthy dose of kink. Please read the content considerations before diving in.

I really hope you love this series, because I have so many ideas for more holiday quickies!

Stay lucky,

Clover 🍀

# WHAT IS OMEGAVERSE?

Omegaverse is a subgenre that takes place in an alternate universe loosely based on canid culture. Similar to wolf shifters, they form packs and have a hierarchy, but there are no shifters in my Omegaverse. There are different *designations* of people - most commonly alpha, beta, and omega. Each Omegaverse may have different designations, rules, and lore depending on the author. In this primer the rules will be specific to the universe I created for these characters, and some details may not be the same as you've read before.

Some things most every Omegaverse has in common though are designations (A/B/O), heats, scents, and knots.

## **Alphas**

Alphas are usually the strongest and most dominant members of society. They are usually big and muscular, and some may have more *alpha power* than others. They can *bark* other designations into submission, forcing them to follow their commands. They also have a special feature at the base of their penises called a *knot*. The knot will swell when the alpha orgasms, and if they are having penetrative sex then it will *lock* them inside their partner. Alphas can be driven into a *rut* when overly aroused.

Alphas are often in positions of power and will behave based on their alpha instincts. Their scents are strong and they will bite a partner to *bond* them.

## Betas

Betas are what most people would consider a "regular" person. They are the most common designation in society and aren't as affected by hormones and pheromones. They do not have knots and won't go into a rut.

There are some worlds where betas may be considered less valuable because they are essentially normal humans. In this world, betas are known to be excellent additions to packs because they are level-headed and can balance out the extremes of alphas and omegas.

## Omegas

Omegas are usually the rarest and most valued designation in society. Because of their low numbers, one omega may form a pack with several alphas and betas. Omegas are generally submissive and natural caretakers. Omegas have heats where their bodies drive them to breed. They will have insatiable sexual appetites and they may need several partners to satisfy them. If omegas are not knotted during their heat, it can be extremely painful and sometimes dangerous for the omega.

In some worlds, omegas may be considered the lowest rung of society, and even like property. They could be barred from getting jobs or may be otherwise controlled by their families or their alphas. They can be any gender and sometimes assigned male at birth (AMAB) people can get pregnant.

## Heats and Ruts

This is a state where omegas and alphas are completely driven by their hormones to copulate. The heat could be on a regular schedule much like a woman's period, or they could be unpredictable. Both options are common tropes in the genre. When in a heat or rut, omegas will often beg for a *bonding bite*, and alphas are driven to *bite* and *claim* their omegas.

These episodes may be controlled by *heat suppressants* or *rut blockers*.

## Scent Matches

Scent is super important in Omegaverse. Everyone has some type of scent, everything from sandalwood to strawberry shortcake and more. Alphas and omegas will have the strongest scents, and betas will have milder scents. When someone finds someone with a scent that is utterly irresistible, they are *scent matches*. This is akin to fated mates. Some universes will have different levels of scent matches (scent sympathetic, scent match, soul scent, etc).

Often if there is an incompatible alpha or omega, then they will smell terrible to the main characters. Usually their scents can indicate mood, souring or burning when they are upset, or sweeter when they are aroused. Mates will often *scent mark* each other by rubbing their *scent glands* or cheeks along the other's skin to *claim* each other.

## Mates/Bonding

As you read above, scent matches often indicate mates. When an alpha claims a beta or omega, they will bite them to mark them with a *bonding bite*. The bonds will work differently in each universe, but most commonly bonded mates will have a two way mental connection where they can sense each other's moods. Sometimes alphas will force bonds on people who are not their willing mates, and sometimes you have to accept the connection for a bond to stick. Sometimes only the alphas need to make the bite, but sometimes both partners need to claim each other to complete the bond. This is probably the most varied tenet in Omegaverse and it doesn't mean any one is incorrect.

# CONTENT CONSIDERATIONS

This is an adult story with explicit sexual content. It's more smut than plot. Like, way more. The characters in this story are polyamorous and have different relationships with each other. That's my nice way of saying everyone is boinking everyone.

In addition to handsome billionaires, you will find fingering, penetrative sex, cunnilingus, fellatio, knotting, face fucking, degradation, rough sex, unprotected sex, questionable use of champagne, and hand necklaces.

You ever look around and wonder, how the hell did I get here? Up until this point, I've never had that experience. I've always played it safe. Followed the rules. Been a good girl—and not in the sexy way.

But as I stand here in the foyer of the historic Manaway House, I'm finally wondering: how the hell did I get here?

I'm awestruck as I take in the sheer opulence around me. The floors are polished marble, the reflection so intense I could probably touch up my makeup in them. An imperial staircase gracefully rises in twin arcs, meeting in the center at a landing that overlooks the entryway. Plush red carpet waterfalls down the steps, daring and bold. In the center of the foyer is a round marble table, a huge ornate floral arrangement dominating the top. My heels click across the tiles until I'm steps away from the art piece. I can't help but admire it.

Bright blooms juxtapose the swaths of white surrounding them. Neon Birds of Paradise interspersed among bold red Anthuriums and hot pink ginger. Dendrobium orchid sprays drape in chaotic elegance.

"Beautiful, isn't it?" The deep, gravelly voice makes me jump. I turn, hand on my heart, only to lay eyes on the most devastating man I've ever seen.

His dark suit is tailored to perfection, a crisp white shirt unbuttoned at the collar giving the illusion of casualness. The skin peeking through is tanned and smooth, and I can't help but follow it up the strong line of his throat to a jaw that could cut glass. Clean shaven without a hint of that five o'clock shadow most men get. His plush lips are quirked into a half smirk, half smile, but it's his eyes that arrest me. Twin pools of the brightest emerald stare at me, and I swear they are burrowing into my soul. This man can't be real.

But there he is, not a figment of my imagination, standing with one hand in his pocket looking like he just stepped off the pages of GQ. He chuckles. "Sorry, I didn't mean to scare you, love. I'm Adrian."

Are you fucking kidding me? He's British, too? I missed the accent when he first spoke, but now it's loud and clear and sends my heart pattering. Honestly, it isn't fair this man is extremely hot, obviously rich, and also has an accent to drive anyone wild. Could he leave anything for us mere mortals to have?

I realize while I've been standing here gaping, Adrian has extended a hand for me to shake. When I get my shit together, I place my hand in his, but instead of pumping it up and down, he brings my knuckles to his lips and places a gentle kiss on my skin. My body warms, and not just from self-consciousness. My clit tingles like he touched me much more intimately and I suck in a breath. That's when his scent hits me. Warm vanilla laced with undertones of suede wraps around me.

*Alpha.*

*Mine.*

Oh, holy fuck. Where did that come from? Never in my life have I had a reaction to an alpha like this. I can't decide if I want to run to him or run away. That's not entirely true. If I listened to my omega instincts, I'd already be wrapped around Adrian like a feral spider monkey, begging him to knot me.

Adrian's eyes are wide. He must be feeling the same electricity I am. His jaw slackens and he takes a step forward, which triggers my fight or flight instinct. And let's just say, I'm not a fighter.

I spin on my heel and run.

"Omega!" Adrian calls after me, but I'm already racing out of the foyer. That's when I realize I didn't even tell him my name. I push through a set of double doors and stop, leaning my back against the cool wall while I catch my breath.

"Who do you think you are, Talia? Cinderella?" I scold myself. "Running away from the hottest, best smelling alpha you've ever met like your ass is on fire. Doing great at your New Year's resolution already." I shake my head in shame.

This year, instead of the usual eat healthier or better work-life-balance resolutions, I promised myself and the universe that I would be bold. I want to shake up my life. Find some excitement. Maybe even love. I want to say yes more often than I say no. Yes to adventure. Yes to new experiences. Yes, yes, *yes*.

Instead, when faced with a sexy alpha who made my whole body tingle, I didn't just say no—I fled the scene. *Pathetic*.

When my breathing returns to normal and I'm sure I haven't been followed, I take in my surroundings. I'm no longer enveloped by glittering opulence like I was in the foyer. Instead, I've wandered into a back hallway, obviously outside the bounds of where guests are expected to go.

The lighting is dim, making the empty corridor a little unsettling. Deep maroon and gold striped paper lines the walls. The kind that's thick and textured and definitely not the peel-and-stick stuff I have in my apartment. Strategically placed art adorns the walls and given the wealth on display everywhere else, I'm assuming they are original pieces. A small wall sconce above each painting shines a bright light downward to highlight the art.

Before I overthink it, I wander down the hall in awe, examining each one. Whoever the collector is, they don't seem to have any one style. Impressionist paintings are mixed in with modern art. A surrealist landscape follows a regal family portrait. There doesn't seem to be any rhyme or reason—and I love it.

I'm admiring a piece that looks like it was done by that one famous street artist, Spanksy, when a thump and a moan pull my focus. My head whips toward the sound and my heart stops.

Oh. My. Gods.

# Levi

"**O**omph." My breath is forced from my lungs as my back hits the wall. Xander dragged me back here under the pretense of a security issue, but based on the fact he's now licking up the side of my neck I'd say that was a farce. Not that I'm complaining. We've been entertaining guests I don't really give a shit about for hours. Thank fuck we only open our mansion once a year.

Xander's warm breath skims my lobe as he growls in my ear, "You seem tense, muffin." Before I can reprimand him for using that stupid pet name, he snakes his hand between us and palms my rapidly stiffening cock through my slacks. I moan in surprise and a sharp inhale sounds, but it didn't come from Xander.

My eyes dart to the right, tracing the sound. A woman stands about twenty feet down the hall, wide eyes locked on us. She's fucking stunning. Pitch black silk drapes elegantly over her curves, the dress somehow teasing and tantalizing at the same time. When she doesn't move to leave, I slide a hand into Xander's hair and grip the strands, roughly turning his head so I can whisper in his ear. "It looks like we have an audience, X."

Xander pulls out of my grasp and gives me a wicked smirk, mischief sparkling in his eyes. He doesn't even glance her way before he replies. "Guess we should give them a show then, huh?"

He slides his palms down my body as he drops to his knees, wasting no time reaching for my belt. He drags his tongue along my waistband as he undoes the buckle and rips open my fly. I dart a quick glance toward our sexy little voyeur, and she's still watching, her chest rising and falling rapidly.

Normally I wouldn't involve a stranger in our play, but this is our house, in the back hall where guests shouldn't be, and she could leave at any time. Instead, her gaze follows Xander as he drops to the floor. He shimmies my slacks down enough that my cock springs free, precum already pearling at the tip. The scent of pink champagne and strawberries hits me, tinged with the sweet note of arousal. *Omega* arousal.

"Oh, fuck!" I nearly shout when Xander deepthroats my cock all the way to my already swelling knot. He's slurping and sucking me with a fervor that surprises me. My cock hits the back of his throat and he gags slightly, but he just pulls back and tries again, taking me deeper on his next dive. My cockhead pushes into his throat and he swallows around me. "Godsdamn, Xan. Are you trying to set a world record for making me come?"

When he looks up at me, his pupils are blown. The black nearly eclipses his irises until there's barely a thin ring left of his ocean blue eyes. Champagne and strawberries hit me again, and I realize he smells her, and it's pushing him to the edge of feral as he devours me. I thread my fingers back into his hair, slowing him down before he makes me embarrass myself. Meeting his gaze, I rumble, "you smell her, too, don't you, X. That pretty little omega's slick must be dripping down her thighs as strong as her scent is." His eyes roll to the back of his head, but he doesn't stop sucking me off. "You like showing off for her, don't you? Want her to see what a hungry cockslut you are." He moans around my cock in answer.

Xander puts his palms on my thighs, his signal to let me know he wants me to fuck his face. With a growl, I grip his head harder, holding it in place as I thrust in and out of his hot mouth. His hips grind in the air, seeking friction for his aching cock. Friction he won't get. Not like this. Like the good boy he is, though, he doesn't reach for his dick. Just lets out needy whimpers as drool leaks down his chin. He's so messy, just how I like him.

I can hear the omega panting, telling me she's still watching. Still enjoying our lewd display. It emboldens me, so I speak louder this time. "How wet do you think her sweet little pussy is, Xan? Mmm screw champagne at midnight. Imagine licking up all that delicious slick instead." The omega whines and I snap my gaze back to hers.

"I'm gonna come, X," I warn just before I thrust deep and hold his face tight to my pelvis. My orgasm slams into me and I spill cum down his throat, all while keeping steady eye contact with our little voyeur omega. He taps my thigh and I let him up. He gasps for air but doesn't stop licking my shaft clean. I tear my gaze from the stunning woman watching to focus back on the alpha at my feet. "Don't you dare waste a drop," I growl.

He doesn't. He never does. When my cock is thoroughly cleaned I yank him to his feet and crush my mouth to his, tasting myself on his tongue. The rapid fire click of heels on tile echoes in the otherwise quiet hall. We end the kiss and watch as the omega in the black dress beats a hasty retreat.

Xander chuckles. "It's cute she thinks she can get away from us after that little stunt."

"I don't mind her playing a little hard-to-get. I smile as I tuck my still half-hard dick back in my slacks and right my clothes. "Do you want me to make you come or do you want to see if we can catch her?"

That wicked smile tips his lips again. "I think I fancy a little hunt."

# Talia

I'm running. Again.

Except this time it's for a totally valid reason. What the fuck was I thinking watching an intimate moment like that? I should have turned and left as soon as I realized what was happening. That was their private time!

Except...

The large alpha knew I was there. He locked eyes with me as his partner dropped to his knees and took him in his mouth. It was like I was frozen in place. Is there such a thing as so horny you can't move? Because if so, that's definitely what happened.

I perfumed like crazy watching the two of them. They had to have noticed because as soon as I did, scents of citrus and clove swelled to match. There was something woodsy, too. Teak, maybe? I was too focused on the messy blow job to nail down the details of their scents. Christ, I don't even know which scents belonged to which man, but it doesn't matter because the effect of them combined was devastating.

Fuck a duck. That was the single hottest moment of my life, and I didn't even come.

Two sets of heavy footsteps sound from behind me and I panic. Oh my gods. They're pissed. They're chasing me down and I'm gonna get arrested for public indecency, and I can't have that on my record. Except, I guess it would be them committing the act. I don't know what you call what I did.

Doesn't matter. I need to get out of here and never show my face on this side of town again. Actually, I should probably move. Yeah, that's the way to go. I've got a cousin in Des Moines I've been meaning to get closer to. Maggie... Mollie? See? I need to spend more time with family. I'll just call a car and have them take me straight to the airport so my embarrassed ass can escape as soon as possible.

The footsteps get louder, and this time when I glance back, I can see them. Fuck. Fuck, fuck, fuc—

My internal berating is cut off as I slam into a wall. No, not a wall. A chest. My heels slip on the slick tile and I brace for impact, but I never hit the ground. Strong arms wrap around me and haul me back up before I can bust my ass. Vanilla and suede tickle my nostrils.

*Oh, no. No no no no no.*

I know who it is before I look, but I need to confirm the full extent of my mortification. Reluctantly dragging my gaze up, bright emerald eyes meet mine and I wish I could melt into the floor to avoid the next-level awkwardness that's about to occur.

Adrian smiles, but doesn't let me go. "We meet again, omega."

# Adrian

I'm not sure which fates are smiling on me today, but I send up my thanks to whoever's got my back. The gorgeous little omega that ran from me earlier literally just fell into my arms, and she smells like strawberries and sin.

Orange and clove hit my senses, followed shortly by weathered teak and petrichor. I jerk my gaze up in surprise, only to confirm that my packmates are here. Levi and Xander are jogging toward us, looking disheveled and smelling like sex. The way their scents mix with the sweet fruit of the omega in my arms—holy gods. It's ambrosia.

The woman I'm holding tenses, then presses her hands to my chest, stammering out an apology. "Oh, gods. I-I'm so sorry! I...uh..." She trails off as she frantically looks between me and my packmates, her sweet scent marred by the sourness that indicates she's stressed. Her cheeks are flushed bright red and her breaths are shallow. When I glance back at my quickly approaching packmates, a lightbulb goes off in my head.

I grip her chin gently and turn her face to mine. "Oh, sweet little one, did you play with my mates?" Of course, I can tell from her scent that she didn't touch either of them, but I love to tease. Her head shakes side to side rapidly. "Mmmm," I rumble, "so you just watched the show."

Her arousal comes back full force and I nearly buckle at the knees as I'm surrounded by strawberries and champagne.

"And what a show it was," Levi says as he finally reaches us. "Xander here was in a particularly giving mood, and you know how he enjoys an audience."

Levi doesn't hesitate to slide up behind the omega, pressing against her back with his chest to sandwich her between us. He leans down to stage whisper in her ear. "It's ok, omega. You didn't do anything wrong. It was fucking hot having you here." He punctuates the sentiment with a nip to her soft lobe and she practically melts back into him.

Xander chooses that moment to push up against all three of us from the side, wrapping his palm around the back of her neck. His thumb brushes over her pulse point as he snares her attention. "You smell so fucking good, omega. You smell like *mine*."

Possessive instincts flare inside me, sharp and swift, and I realize he's right. She does smell like mine. *Ours*.

She's our scent match.

"You feel it, too, don't you beautiful?" Xander continues.

She bites her lower lip in a way that I don't think is meant to be teasing, but it is all the same. She nods shyly then whispers so quietly I almost miss it despite her being pressed against me. "Y-yes."

That's all it takes to make my libido jump to the next level, my cock somehow stiffening even more. A rusty purr rattles in my chest, and it feels so right. Xander releases her chin as she looks at me, eyes glazed with lust and comfort. "What's your name, love?"

I can't believe it's taken this long before we even know what to call our soulmate. But in my defense, she did run away from me like she was an Olympic sprinter a little while ago.

"Talia," she murmurs. Levi spins her to face him, pushing a knee between her thighs. She instinctively rolls her hips, seeking friction for what has to be her slick as fuck clit. "Now we know what to call you as we take turns worshiping your tight little body."

I'm about to chastise him for being so forward, but it's like a switch flips in our little omega. Her shoulders straighten and she locks gazes with Levi before bringing her thumb to his lips. He opens for her, sucking the digit in his mouth. After a moment, she slides it out, dragging the pad across his lower lip, making it bounce roughly when she releases it.

Her voice is sultry when she finally speaks. "And are you gonna tell me what names I'll be screaming out later?"

Levi's grin is cocky as he replies. "My name is Levi, sugar. But I also respond to Sir, god, and daddy."

Fuck. I've never been into the daddy thing, but imagining Talia whining it while she writhes on my knot and I pump her full of my cum is really doing it for me right now. A stiff breeze would make me bust in my pants like an untried pup at this point.

My last packmate gently wraps his fingers around Talia's throat and licks a slow line along her jaw. "And I'm Xander. I don't want you to call me daddy, but I wouldn't complain if you called me your good boy."

I nearly do come in my slacks as Talia's perfume explodes. A crash coming from the industrial kitchen pops the horny bubble we've been trapped in for the last few minutes. Suddenly, I'm reminded we aren't alone. Hundreds of guests are milling around the mansion and gardens just outside. A growl builds in my throat when I think about any of those fuckers scenting Talia, or worse, seeing her hot and disheveled for us.

"We need to go upstairs," I snarl, turning Talia back to me. "What do you think, omega? Can we take you upstairs and show you how to ring in the new year properly?"

# 5

## Xander

I'm dead.

I've died and gone to heaven. That's the only explanation for what's happening right now. An hour ago, I was dragging Levi out of the ballroom to suck his dick. Now I'm staring at my gloriously naked scent-matched omega as she presents her perfect pussy to our pack. Her taste lingers on my lips, making me want to go back for more. When she spreads her legs further apart, I get a glimpse of her tight, puckered hole and decide I want to lick her there instead.

Before I can, Talia snakes a hand between her thighs and rubs her swollen clit. "Please, alpha. I need you."

Adrian shifts, pressing his chest to my back and wrapping his muscular arms around my torso. One hand slides up my body to settle on my throat, the other heads the opposite direction to dip into the waistband of my slacks.

"You heard our omega, Levi. Don't keep her waiting." Adrian's hand wraps around my cock and pumps roughly, the way he knows I like. His accent makes everything he says sound five times dirtier. "X and I are going to watch you take her apart."

Levi strips in no time and slides behind our omega on his knees, lining up his cock with her slick entrance. He doesn't tease her this time, just slams in deep right up to his knot.

"Fuck! You're huge!" Talia cries out, and we all freeze.

"I'm so sorry, omega. Are you okay?" Levi looks stricken and tries to pull out of her but she reaches back to hold him in place.

"I didn't say it was a bad thing. Don't you dare pull out. I need you to *move*. Fuck me hard, alpha." This woman is amazing. They tell you a scent match is supposed to be your perfect mate, but I never could have imagined Talia in my wildest dreams.

Levi growls and begins fucking Talia in earnest, his grip on her hips bruising. Our omega squirms and moans in pleasure, but after a moment she whines like she needs something more. "Do you want Xander to fill your mouth, omega? His cock is weeping for you."

"Yes! Yes, yes yes!" Talia screams, and I can't tell if it's from what Levi is doing to her or because she wants my dick. Doesn't really matter. I've already kicked my pants off and am stalking toward the bed, sliding in front of our omega and bracketing my thighs around her head. When my cock's in range, she lunges forward and takes my cock to the back of her throat. She bobs her head in sync with Levi's thrusts, going deeper each time he fucks her forward. She claws at my shirt, so I rip it off with one hand and toss it somewhere to the side.

Adrian has migrated to a plush chair in the corner of the room, stroking himself slowly as he observes like a king. Fitting for the leader of our pack. I'd make a cuck-chair joke, but we all know he's just biding his time until he gets his turn with Talia. The vision we make is obscene. The three of us, naked and tangled in each other while Adrian is still in his tux, only his cock on display.

"Fuck, shes strangling my cock, Levi grits out. "I'm not gonna last. Can I come inside you, omega? I want to fill up your perfect cunt until you're bulging."

Talia pops off my cock for a moment to reply. "Yes! Give it to me. Knot me, alpha!" She dives back down with fervor and Levi's thrusts become erratic. He reaches around to stroke her clit as he pops his knot into her channel, and she screams around my cock as she comes. Levi's hips still as he reaches his own peak, and I'm not far behind.

"Omega, I'm almost there. If you don't want a mouthful you need to—" I'm cut off by her wrapping her little fist around my knot and squeezing hard. That sends me careening over the edge into my own climax, and our perfect mate swallows every single drop.

I reluctantly pull out of her warm mouth and Levi gently maneuvers them to lie on their sides. He promptly pulls her tight to his chest, wrapping her tight like she's the most precious thing on this earth. The bed vibrates and I'm confused for a moment until I realize he's softly purring for her. Shock hits me before a feeling of rightness settles. I've never heard him purr for anyone but me or Adrian. We've shared women before, even dated a couple omegas, but this is different. *She's* different.

Following my instincts, I slip down the bed until I'm aligned with Talia's front, pushing in close and rattling out my own purr for our soulmate.

## 6

L evi's knot slips out of my pussy, a mixture of my slick and his cum dripping down my thighs and ass. He gets out of bed then heads toward a door I assume is a bathroom, and I roll onto my back. Xander grumbles as I push up out of his arms onto my elbows. Adrian is still fully clothed, his eyes full of heat locked on me.

Cheers suddenly erupt from downstairs, so loud we can hear the ruckus all the way up here. A modern clock on the bedside table shows it's midnight. We officially rang in the new year with a bang. I chuckle at my own joke until Adrian stands and walks across the room like a predator. My inner omega is instantly alert.

Levi comes back with a warm towel and cleans me gently, but I can't focus on anything but their pack leader and what he's doing. Confusion and then a tinge of rejection hit me when he walks right past me. I rip my stare from him, refusing to be *that* omega, until I hear the loud, distinctive *pop* of a cork. Adrian makes his way to the bed carrying a bottle of champagne, wisps of fog escaping the glass neck. He sends the other two alphas a look and they silently stand, leaving me alone in the center of the sheets. Willing prey.

"It looks like a toast is in order. What do you think, little one?" he purrs.

"I think you're missing something essential for a toast," I note, looking pointedly at his lack of glassware. He chuckles wicked and low.

"Oh, I was thinking we'd share this champagne another way." He brings the rim to his lips and takes a swig directly from the bottle. He swallows the first gulp, but then holds the second in his mouth. He tilts my chin up as he leans over me, and I open my mouth eagerly. Groans come from Levi and Xander who are off to the side, but Adrian's eyes light up with lust and his scent blooms with arousal. He slowly dribbles the champagne onto my tongue, not stopping until it escapes the corner of my lips and drips down my chin.

"Swallow." The single word command falls from his lips and I comply immediately, drinking down the sweet bubbly liquid. "Good girl."

Well, fuck. That's definitely as good as they say it is in the romance novels I read.

Adrian takes another sip as he drags his gaze down my body appreciatively. The way all three of these men look at me gives me confidence I didn't know was possible. I feel sexy and desired. Worthy.

Adrian's eyes lock onto my breasts, and he dips down to take a taut nipple into his mouth. I jerk as the cold liquid surrounds my hot flesh. Tiny bubbles pop against my skin, the sensation tingly and pleasant. The tip of his tongue flicks over the peak before he sucks and swallows. He kisses across my chest to repeat the move on my other breast. The slow tease is a drastic change of pace from the hard and fast way his packmates took me, but it's not unwelcome.

The pack leader stands and eyes Levi and Xander before tipping the bottle over my chest. Goosebumps rise as the cold champagne drips over my tits and down my ribs. It isn't long before hot tongues are tracing the trails of liquid, Levi and Xander lapping up the rivulets until they each settle over a breast to lick and tease my nipples once more.

Cold hits my skin again. This time Adrian drips champagne down my sternum, letting it run down my stomach to pool in my navel. Levi abandons my nipple to chase the new path, tongue dipping into my belly button to lap up the excess. The constant switching between hot and cold have my body on edge, unable to predict which sensation is coming next.

I don't realize I've tossed my head back until a cool sensation on my clit has me whipping it back up to see what they're doing to me. Sure enough, Adrian has the bottle tipped over my mound. It's unbelievably hot. I definitely won't be able to look at a glass of champagne without blushing ever again.

Adrian smirks and takes a large swig of champagne, then lowers to my eager pussy. When he wraps his lips around my clit with the bubbly still in his mouth, my hips buck. The alpha teases my swollen nub with this tongue, the effervescence of the alcohol tickling the sensitive nerves. He alternates between sucking and licking until the champagne warms to my body, then he swallows the gulp and pours more into his mouth to repeat the process. His packmates continue to worship my body, hands and tongues everywhere at once.

Adrian suddenly sucks my clit hard, and I come with a cry. He surges up my body to capture my moans with his kisses, and I'm ready to beg this alpha for his knot and his bite. I've never felt this way during sex before, and I don't think it's just because they're my scent matches. Heat licks at my skin, a need building in my empty core I'm desperate for them to fill.

"Please, alpha," I whine, punctuating my plea with a nip to Adrian's bottom lip. Quicker than lightning he flips us, settling me on top of him with our sexes aligned.

"Take what you need, omega. I'm yours."

I hesitate because I've never felt too confident being on top, until my resolution echoes in my mind once more. *Yes. Yes, yes, yes.*

I lift my hips and grip his hard cock, bringing it to my entrance and sinking down his shaft in a smooth stroke. His eyes close and he murmurs a string of curses as I slip right onto his knot. It's not fully engorged yet, so I take advantage. His hands land on my hips and he helps me rise and lower, his knot popping in and out of my pussy.

Fingers slide into my hair, gently encouraging me to turn my head. Levi is there, hard cock dripping precum just in front of my lips. I lick it up eagerly, swirling my tongue around the head. Movement behind him snags my attention, and I gasp as I see Xander's arm moving rhythmically behind Levi's back. Is he doing what I think he's doing?

"Fuck, she just clenched around my cock so hard," Adrian groans. "Does it turn you on knowing Xan is about to fuck Levi's ass while you suck him off, omega?"

I nod rapidly as Xander grips Levi's hip, pushing into him slowly. Levi closes his eyes and lets out a hiss, pushing his ass back toward Xander, seeking more. I want to contribute to his pleasure, so I don't hesitate to lean over and take Levi's cock back in my mouth. Levi growls and pops his eyes open to stare at me in approval, then reaches around to play with my clit.

We're a writhing mass of sweat-slicked skin, everyone giving and receiving pleasure the way only scent-matches can. Time ceases to exist as we get lost in each other until Adrian's knot is too large for me to bounce on. He pushes deep, locking his knot inside me while he continues to rut shallowly up into me. I don't think. I act on pure instinct. I rip my mouth from Levi's cock and sink my teeth into his hip. The copper tang of blood coats my tongue as a partial bond forms. Levi shouts when his release hits him and he paints my tits with his spend.

# 7

## Talia

"Did she just..." Xander trails off when he sees me licking my bite, tending to the wound.

"She sure fucking did." Levi confirms before he grips my hair and yanks my head back, exposing my throat. "*Mine*," he growls as he sinks his teeth in where my neck meets my shoulder. The bond snaps into place, complete with both our bites. Levi's shock mirrors my own, but adoration and awe also float down the bond.

Not to be left out, Xander reaches around Levi to grasp my wrist so he can bring my hand to his mouth. He sinks his teeth into the fleshy spot between my thumb and forefinger a moment later, igniting another bond in my soul. He licks over the punctures to seal them, then offers me his arm. I take it greedily, sucking the soft skin on the bottom of his forearm into my mouth before I bite.

"Oh fuck, baby girl. I feel you. I-I can't..." Xander trails off as his hips still, flush against Levi's. With the bond complete, his pleasure ricochets through me, too, tipping me over the edge into ecstasy again.

When my head stops spinning, I realize Adrian has

stilled beneath me. He's staring at me, and I can't tell if his expression is good or bad. Did I fuck up? I acted on instinct, and they bit me back, but we obviously didn't talk about it beforehand.

Xander and Levi pull apart and stumble to the bed, flopping onto the mattress near the headboard. I dart a nervous glance between them and their pack lead, unsure if I should apologize, even if I don't want to.

"*Mine!*" The tension breaks when Adrian does. He rolls us until he's on top, hooking my legs over his shoulders. He pushes forward, my knees hitting my chest, my body squished like a pretzel as he grinds into me. The angle allows him to get impossibly deep. Each thrust drags his thick knot along my g-spot. He's relentless and damn near feral. If I was in heat, I'd think he was lost to a rut, but I'm not. If he's this aggressive outside of my heat, I can't wait to see what he unleashes on me when a true rut takes over.

We're reduced to nothing but grunts and moans. Sweaty skin and frantic kisses. His cock swells inside of me as he roars his release, hot lashes of cum filling me. I expect to feel his teeth, but he holds back, a silent question in his eyes.

I try to convey my need and earnestness as I lock my gaze with his. "Yes. Bite me, alpha. P-please. Bite!"

He strikes fast as a snake, searing his mark along my neck on the opposite side of Levi's. I come so hard I see stars and nearly black out. When I come to, my teeth are buried in Adrian's neck, giving him a matching bite.

We collapse, spent, into a pile where everyone is touching me in some way. Possessive. Perfect. No one speaks for a while as we soak in the gravity of what we've just done.

"I can hear you over thinking from here, little one."

Adrian rumbles. "You're ours now, love. And we're never letting you go."

Agreement floats down the bonds from all three alphas, reassurance from my new pack exactly what I needed. For once, I don't over analyze. Pushing myself out of my comfort zone and saying yes to my instincts brought me my scent matches. It's unconventional, but I wouldn't have it any other way.

I'm eager to discover what the future will bring me—us —the next time we choose to say yes.

Yes, yes, yes.

## ABOUT THE AUTHOR

Clover Holloway is the cozier side of Unfortunate Reads, writing steamy monster and omegaverse romance that will make you swoon and sweat.

A long time romance reader turned author, she just can't help but make her stories cozy. She's an ADHD agent of chaos so her book topics may vary wildly, but you can always expect an HEA. She's an avid fan of traditional millennial customs including craft breweries, monstera plants, and skinny jeans.

Get lucky at cloverholloway.com.

## ALSO BY CLOVER HOLLOWAY

### Welcome to Bone Town

Adventure Omegaverse co-written with Thea Masen

---

### Knot Letting Go

Olympic Omegaverse co-written with Thea Masen

---

### Unwrapping the Pack

*Part of the Omegaverse Holiday Quickies series*

---

### Slip into Me

A short eel-shifter, fated mates novella.

*Originally published in the Strange Love charity anthology.*

---

### Taking a Tumble

Meet cute with a dad-bod demon pet shop owner and a curvy, confident human woman.

*Part of the Ghostlight Falls series.*

---

## Zero to 69

A sentient object shifter romance co-written with Thea Masen &
Kate McDarris